JASON S

043455

FULL MOON
HORROR

Illustrated by Alberto Dal Lago

STONE ARCH BOOKS
a capstone imprint

Jason Strange is published by
Stone Arch Books
A Capstone Imprint
151 Good Counsel Drive, P.O. Box 669
Mankato, Minnesota 56002
www.capstonepub.com

Copyright © 2012 by Stone Arch Books

Library of Congress Cataloging-in-Publication Data is available at the Library of
Congress website.

Summary: When his brother's car runs out of gas late at night, thirteen-year-old Jack
Kipping and his friends are stranded on a lonely road--and the moon is full.

ISBN 978-1-4342-3235-9 (library binding)
ISBN 978-1-4342-3434-6 (pbk.)

Art Director/Graphic Designer: Kay Fraser
Production Specialist: Michelle Biedscheid

Photo credits:
Shutterstock: Nikita Rogul (handcuffs, p. 2); Stephen Mulcahey (police badge, p. 2);
B&T Media Group (blank badge, p. 2); Picsfive (coffee stain, pp. 2, 5, 12, 17, 24, 30,
42, 48, 57); Andy Dean Photography (paper, pen, coffee, pp. 2, 66); osov (blank notes,
p. 1); Thomas M Perkins (folder with blank paper, pp. 66, 67); M.E. Mulder (black
electrical tape, pp. 5, 9, 18, 23, 33, 37, 43, 47, 53, 60, 69, 70, 71)

Printed in the United States of America in Stevens Point, Wisconsin.
032011
006111WZF11

TABLE OF CONTENTS

- Chapter 1: Wiped Out -

Jack Kipping was exhausted. He slouched in the passenger seat of his brother's car as it zipped down the highway toward home.

"I shouldn't have taken that swim this morning," Jack said. "I'm wiped out."

His older brother Paul smiled. "I told you," he said. "You must have swum ten miles in the lake this weekend."

Jack nodded and rubbed his sore shoulders.

Jack's friends Nelson and Zeek lounged in the backseat. "Yeah, Jack," Zeek said. "You better not have worn yourself out too much."

"That's right," Nelson said. "We've got track tryouts this week."

"I'll be fine," Jack said. "Don't worry about me."

They passed a sign that said "Now Leaving Ravens Pass." The car jerked forward suddenly. Then it turned off and rolled to a stop.

"What was that?" Nelson asked. He leaned forward between the two front seats.

"I have no idea," Paul said. He turned the key in the ignition, but nothing happened.

Jack pointed at the dashboard. "Um, you're out of gas, you ninny," he told Paul. "Don't you know what 'E' means?"

"Oh, no. I thought we had plenty," Paul said. He dropped his head back on the seat. "I can't believe I did that!"

"I can," Nelson said under his breath.

"Ha-ha," Paul said. He took the keys out of the car. "I'll walk back to that gas station we passed about a mile back."

"Yeah, we'll wait here," Jack said. "I think I've had more than enough exercise for one weekend."

"Agreed," Zeek said.

"I'm taking my keys," Paul said. "That means no radio, no lights. It's going to be dark soon."

"So walk fast," Jack said. "We'll be fine, anyway. It's a full moon tonight. Should be nice and bright."

Paul shook his head and got out of the car. Then he opened the trunk and got the gas can. Soon he was headed down the road toward the gas station.

After a minute, Nelson flicked Jack in the ear. "Hey, what was that for?" Jack asked.

Nelson shrugged and said, "I don't know. I'm bored."

– Chapter 2: Fresh Air –

After twenty minutes, Paul wasn't back yet. "It's getting hot in here," Zeek said. He kicked the back of Jack's seat. "Open the window."

"I can't!" Jack said. He turned in his seat to face Zeek and Nelson and added, "Paul took the keys, remember? The windows won't open without keys."

"Well, I need some air," Zeek said. He opened his door and got out.

"Me too," Nelson said. He stepped out to and stretched his arms.

Jack sighed. "Fine," he said. Then he got out too and closed his door. "One of you leave your door open, though," he said . . . just as both the back doors closed.

"Oops," Zeek said.

"Why?" Nelson said. "They're not locked."

As he said it, the locks clicked.

"They lock on their own," Jack said. He leaned against the car. "Great, now we're locked out of the car."

Zeek patted him on the shoulder. "Big deal," Zeek said. "Your bro will be back in a few minutes. Then he'll open the doors."

Jack nodded. "I guess," he said. "It's not like it's raining."

Just then, a big drop splattered against the car hood with a loud ping.

"This is your fault, Jack," Nelson said. "You had to say it's wasn't raining."

The skies opened up. It began to pour. Thunder cracked and lightning burned across the sky. The torrent of rain was deafening.

"We have to find shelter!" Zeek shouted.

The other boys nodded. "I'm pretty sure there was an overpass, not far back," Jack said. "We can run for it."

The three boys sprinted along the shoulder of the highway. "There," Jack called out. They reached the overpass and stopped. As soon as he was out of the rain, Jack bent, with his hands on his knees, to catch his breath. "I hurt all over," he said.

The other boys laughed, but they were out of breath too.

"It can't rain like this for too long," Nelson said. He sat down on the curb, just under cover, and watched the pouring rain fall.

Zeek and Jack sat next to him. Jack grabbed his shirt and rung out some of the water.

"I'm soaked to the skin," he said. "I might as well have gone swimming in my clothes."

The other boys laughed. Then Nelson spotted someone walking down the road. "Hey, is that Paul?" he asked. From where they sat, and with the sun nearly all the way down, it was hard to be sure.

"I hope so," Zeek said. He stood up and waved his arms. "Hey, Paul!" he called out.

Jack grabbed his wrist and pulled him back down. "He doesn't have a gas can, whoever that is," Jack said. "That's not Paul."

"Oh, whoops," Zeek said.

The figure stopped a moment. Then the person seemed to realize where the boys were sitting. He started jogging quickly toward them.

"Well, here he comes," Jack said. "I hope he's not a crazy murderer or something."

"Don't be ridiculous," Nelson said. The figure got closer. "See?" Nelson went on. "He's our age."

Zeek nodded. "Nothing to be afraid of," he said. Then, facing the stranger, he said, "Over here. Looking for shelter from the rain?"

The guy stepped under the overpass. He looked about their age — maybe a year or so older — and his clothes were soaking wet. His pant legs were both torn at the ankles.

"Hey, are you okay?" Jack asked. "You look like you've been walking for a long time."

The boy smiled at Jack and his friends. "Not that long," he said. "I'm sure glad I found this overpass before it got much darker. I'd hate to get lost in those woods."

He nodded toward the forest just off the highway. Jack, Nelson, and Zeek glanced at the woods. They were creepy looking, dark and deep.

"Can I join you?" the boy asked.

Jack and his friends looked at each other. Then Jack answered, "Sure."

The boy sat down and took a deep breath. "Thanks," he said. "I'm exhausted. My name is Caleb, by the way."

Jack introduced himself and his friends. "I'm Jack," he said. "Those two yahoos are Zeek and Nelson."

Caleb smiled. "You guys don't have any food, do you?" he asked. "I feel like I could eat a horse."

"Sorry," Jack said. "All our snacks are in the car."

"You have a car?" Caleb asked. "Why are you sitting here, then?"

"We ran out of gas," Zeek explained. "Jack's brother went to get gas back down the road."

"And we got locked out of the car," Nelson added.

Caleb nodded. "Well, no big deal," he said. "Soon the big full moon will be out. Then everything will seem a little brighter."

"What's that mean?" Jack asked. But Caleb didn't answer. He just looked at his hand and picked his dirty fingernails.

- Chapter 3: The Animal In Me -

"This is ridiculous," Zeek said. "Your brother has been gone for, like, an hour." He stood up and walked to the other side of the overpass.

"Yeah, what's taking so long, anyway?" Nelson asked.

Jack didn't answer. He just shrugged. The new boy, Caleb, still sat next to him on the curb. He bit his fingernails and bounced his knee up and down.

"Are you nervous about something?" Jack asked him.

Caleb shook his head and smiled. "Nah," he said. "Just hungry. And I'm excited. I love full moons, don't you?"

Jack watched his friends a few yards away. He wished they hadn't left him sitting there with this weirdo. "Um, I guess," he said. "I never thought about it before. Are you superstitious or something?"

"Nah, nothing like that," Caleb said. "They just really bring out the animal in me." Then he smiled and went back to biting his nails.

"I'm going to see what my friends are doing," Jack said. He got up and walked over to Zeek and Nelson. "Zeek," Jack said, "is your cell phone getting any service?"

Zeek shook his head. "I just tried," he said. "Nothing. What is taking your stupid brother so long?"

"I don't know," Jack said. "But I wish he'd hurry. This guy Caleb is giving me the creeps."

The three boys looked over their shoulders at Caleb. He stood up and waved, then started to pull off his shirt.

"What is he doing now?" Nelson whispered to his friends.

Zeek pointed at the horizon. "The moon is just about up," he said.

Jack whistled. "Wow, it's huge," he said. The full moon came up from the earth like a giant dinner plate, glowing big and bright.

"Hey," Jack called to Caleb, "the moon's out now."

There was no reply. Caleb was nowhere to be seen. The three boys turned around, looking for the new boy. As they did, a huge figure leaped across the overpass.

The figure landed in front of them, its big hairy feet slapping the pavement. It opened its long snout, showing long, sharp teeth and fangs.

Then it roared.

- Chapter 4: Luna -

"Keep running!" Jack shouted. He, Nelson, and Zeek ran down the highway toward the gas station.

"He got me," Zeek said as he ran. Jack noticed he was limping a bit, but he still managed to keep up.

"Where?" Jack asked.

Zeek held his stomach. "Here," he said. In the dark, Jack could only tell the front of his friend's shirt was torn.

"He's catching up," Nelson said, looking back over his shoulder as he ran.

Jack looked back. The werewolf — what else could it be? — ran on all fours. It loped quickly toward them.

"We need to hide," Jack said. He looked to his left, into the dark woods. "We have to go into the woods."

"In there?" Zeek asked, gasping for breath. "No way."

"If we don't hide, he'll catch us in no time," Jack said. He grabbed Zeek's elbow. "Trust me," Jack added.

Nelson took Zeek's other elbow. They guided their wounded friend into the trees.

"This is hopeless," Zeek said. "I can't run anymore."

Jack looked ahead, hoping for any sign of someplace to hide. "There!" he said, pointing ahead with his free arm. "I see a light. It must be a house."

With Nelson and Jack's help, Zeek managed to make it to the light. It was a house after all.

The boys stood in front of the house and looked up at it.

The farmhouse was big and white, but the paint was dirty from years of dust. On the porch was a broken swing, and the screen door opened and slapped closed in the rain and the wind.

"This place is almost as creepy as that monster," Nelson said.

"We can try to find another house," Jack said.

A howl pierced the night. It was followed by a long and low growl.

"This will be fine," Zeek said. He limped onto the porch and banged on the heavy door behind the screen door.

"Hello?!" he called out.

A moment later, the old door swung open. Standing there was an old woman and a girl about the boys' age.

"Hello," the old woman said. "Are you friends of my granddaughter's?"

The girl shook her head. "I don't know these boys, Grandma," she said. "I think they're in trouble."

"We are," Jack said. "Our friend is hurt. Can we please come in and, um, use the phone?"

"Of course, boys," the old woman said.

The old woman stepped to the side. Her granddaughter took Zeek by one arm and helped him in.

"You look terrible," the girl said.

In the light of the entryway, Jack could now see his friend's wound better. His shirt was torn clean through in a ten-inch-long gash. But what was worse, it was soaked with blood.

Jack could see the gash across his friend's stomach. It didn't look deep, but it was bleeding a lot.

"We have to get him cleaned up," the girl said. "Grandma, can you help?"

"Of course," Grandma said. "I haven't forgotten much about my nursing days." The old lady led Zeek away.

"Thank you," Jack said to the girl. "I'm Jack. This is Nelson. The other guy is Zeek."

"Nice to meet you," the girl said. "My name is Luna. Come and sit down. Do you want a soda? Anything?" She pointed at an old-fashioned couch in the front room.

Jack and Nelson shook their heads and sat down. Luna sat across from them in a plain wooden chair. "So what happened?" she asked. "He looked really hurt."

"A wild dog bit him," Nelson said quickly.

Luna looked shocked. "It might have been a bear," Jack said. "It was so dark."

Luna pulled her necklace out of her shirt and fiddled with the charm. Shaking her head slowly, she said, "I've heard about a pack of wild dogs that hangs out near the highway."

"That's where it happened," Jack said. "We ran out of gas. My brother went to get more, but . . . I don't know what's taking him so long."

"Down at Gary's Gas?" the girl asked.

Jack shrugged. "I don't know," he said. "Some place we passed about a mile back."

Luna nodded. "That's Gary's place," she said. "It's the only place to get gas for miles. I'll give him a call." She got up and headed into the other room. Soon the boys heard her talking into the phone.

"Do you think she suspects anything?" Nelson said quietly to Jack.

"You mean, does she know that a werewolf attacked Zeek?" Jack asked.

"So you do think it was a werewolf," Nelson said. "Me too."

Jack nodded. "I knew there was something odd about that guy," he said. "He kept talking about the moon, and his fingernails were super long."

"It's lucky we escaped with our lives," Nelson said.

"I hope Zeek is okay," Jack said.

Luna hung up and came back into the room. "Well, they haven't seen your brother," she said. "Gary said he'll call here if he shows up."

"He never made it?" Jack said. "How can that be? He's been gone for over an hour."

Nelson's face went white and he turned to Jack. "What if the werewolf —," he said, but he cut himself off.

"What?" Luna said. "The werewolf?" She fidgeted with her necklace again.

Jack glared at Nelson. "We might as well tell her now," Jack said.

"Sorry," Nelson said. He looked at his feet.

Jack faced Luna. "We think Zeek was attacked by a werewolf," he said.

Luna glanced at the doorway, then nodded. "Don't mention this in front of Grandma," she said. "She's very superstitious, and she might get upset. But I'll get her to drive us to Gary's. We can look for your brother on the road."

– Chapter 5: The Ride –

Grandma's car was a big old station wagon. The boys and Luna piled in. Luna got in front, and the boys sat together in the backseat. Grandma took off down the road.

The road to the highway was long and windy. It was surrounded by deep woods.

"How's your injury?" Jack asked Zeek.

"Better," Zeek said. "I mean, not great. But Grandma stopped the bleeding."

Luna looked back at Zeek and smiled. "You'll be okay," she said.

A howl filled the night air. It sounded close. Luna went back to fiddling with her necklace and faced forward.

"We're nearly there," Grandma said. "I hope your brother will be there too."

Grandma parked the big station wagon at the pumps and turned off the car.

Jack opened the door and jumped out. He ran for the shop, hoping to see Paul standing there with his gas can.

The only person inside was a teenage employee. He was behind the counter, flipping through a comic book. He didn't even look up until Luna came in.

"Hi, Kenny," she said. "Is Gary around?"

Kenny looked confused. "Gary?" he said. "He has tonight off. You know that."

Luna's eyes went wide, but it was too late. Kenny had exposed her lie.

"The night off?" Jack repeated. He backed away from the girl. "Hey, what is this?"

Zeek and Nelson came inside and joined Jack. Luna smiled at them and put out her hand, inviting Jack to take it. "Don't run away, guys," she said. "It's easier if you just come along with me right now."

Jack shoved his friends toward the door. The three went for the exit just as Grandma came in and blocked it.

"Please," Jack said. "Let us go."

Grandma took a rope from behind her back. "Oh, I'm sorry, dears," she said. "You're never leaving here."

– Chapter 6: Inside the Trap –

"Guys, don't struggle," Luna said from behind them. Kenny came out from behind the counter and grabbed Jack's wrists.

"Jack, is that you?" Paul called out from somewhere in the store.

"Paul!" Jack replied. "Where are you?"

Jack elbowed Kenny in the stomach and broke free. "Let's go," he said to Nelson and Zeek. The three boys darted for a door toward the back of the store.

"It's heavy," Jack said. He tugged on the handle. "Help me!" Zeek and Nelson grabbed the handle too, but it wouldn't budge.

"It's locked," Luna said. She stood next to the boys. "You really can't escape."

"If you don't believe my granddaughter," Grandma said, "take a peek through the window in the door."

Jack glared at her. He got up on his tiptoes and looked in through the window. "It's Paul!" he said. Inside, Paul was hunched in a corner, chained to the wall by his ankles.

"Jack!" Paul said when he spotted his brother at the window. "You have to get me out of here."

Across from Paul was a big iron gate, dividing the dank-looking room in half.

On the other side of the gate, in the corner as far from Paul as possible, a dark figure was curled up.

"Is that . . . ," Jack whispered.

Suddenly the figure sprang from the cement floor. It was huge and covered in hair. It, too, had a chain around its ankle. It saw Jack and tried to jump at the door, but the chain kept it far away. It growled and snarled, then let loose a wicked howl.

"It's the werewolf," Jack said. He spun to face Luna and Grandma. Then he said to Nelson over his shoulder, "They've got the werewolf in there with Paul."

Grandma chuckled. "That isn't the werewolf you saw," she said. She pulled something from her pocket and rubbed it between her thumb and first finger.

"That's the werewolf's father in there," Luna said. "Gary, the gas station owner."

"Gary?" Jack repeated. "Then . . . you knew! You knew who had attacked Zeek all along. You knew my brother was walking into a death trap."

Luna shrugged and smiled. "It's what has to be done," she said as she fiddled with the charm on her necklace. "When they've eaten, the beasts are calm. They don't terrorize Ravens Pass, once they aren't hungry anymore."

"So you're going to feed them my brother?" Jack snapped.

"And you three, as well," Grandma said.

Just then, Kenny appeared behind the three boys. Grandma unlocked the door and swung it open.

Kenny and Luna shoved the three boys, sending them sprawling into the cold cement cell.

Jack got up quickly and went for the door, but it slammed shut in his face. He heard the bolt lock.

Past the gate, the werewolf father paced back and forth, eyeing the boys. His mouth hung open. His big, sharp teeth were shiny with drool and stained by old meat.

The boys were doomed.

- Chapter 7: Family -

"You can't do this!" Jack shouted through the window in the door.

"We must," Luna replied quietly. "Try to understand. If the werewolves do not eat, they terrorize Ravens Pass. This keeps them calm until the full moon has passed."

"But why us?" Nelson called.

"You are not from here," Grandma said. "No one in Ravens Pass will miss you."

"Now we must go," Luna said. "Gary's son — the other werewolf — is still out there. We'll capture him and bring him back. He will have supper with his father."

Jack turned to the others. "These people are crazy," he said.

Paul nodded. "Tell me about it," he said.

Nelson ran to the door. "But if you can catch them," he said, "why don't you just chain them up for good? Don't feed them at all!"

For a moment, there was no reply. Jack and Zeek ran to the door and tried to listen. "Did they leave already?" Zeek said.

"No," Luna said. "We're still here."

"Why won't you answer?" Jack asked. "Why don't you just not feed them at all?"

"Your questions have upset Grandma," Luna said. "If we don't feed the werewolves human meat during the full moon, they'll die."

Nelson shouted back, "So what? Let them die!"

A great sob came from the other side of the door.

"There, there, Grandma," Luna said. "They'll be gone soon." Then her voice got suddenly louder and angry. "You've made Grandma cry," she snapped at the boys. "Don't you see? We can't just let them die!"

"Why not?" Jack asked.

"Because Gary and his son are family," Luna said. "Gary is my uncle. Grandma's son. Caleb is my cousin."

– Chapter 8: The Plan –

"We have to get out of here before they come back with Caleb," Jack said.

Paul groaned. "But how?" he asked.

Jack shook his head, and Zeek went to the window. "Hey, Kenny," Zeek called out.

"Hmm?" said the young guy at the counter. He didn't sound too interested.

"Can't you let us out of here?" Zeek asked. "Gary's not your uncle, right?"

"Nope," Kenny said. "But he is my boss. If he dies, the station will close. I'll be out of a job."

"Real nice," Nelson said. He slumped against the wall next to Paul.

"Sorry, guys," Kenny added. "Nothing I can do."

Then Jack had an idea. He whispered to Zeek, "Follow my lead." Zeek nodded.

"Say, guys," Jack said, loud enough so Kenny would hear. "Look at this cool charm I have." He winked at his friends.

The other boys gathered around, except Paul, who was still chained to the wall. Jack held out his hand, which was empty.

"Wow," Nelson said. "Where'd you get that?"

"I pulled it off that girl's neck," Jack said. "What's her name? Luna?"

"Yup," Zeek said. "I recognize it. It's pretty cool."

Soon the boys heard footsteps coming toward the door. Jack closed his hand and shoved it into his pocket, pretending that he was putting the charm away.

"What are you talking about in there?" Kenny called.

"Oh, nothing," Jack said. He winked at his friends, then nodded toward the door.

The three unchained boys went to the door quietly and stood just to the side.

"Don't lie to me," Kenny said. "Do I seem stupid to you? I heard you say you have Luna's charm. Now hand it over."

"No way," Jack said. "I stole it fair and square. What do you care, anyway?"

"It's important to her," Kenny said. "Toss it through the window and I won't tell anyone you stole it."

"If you want it," Jack said, "come on in and take it."

"Okay, you asked for it," Kenny said. "I'm coming in. And don't try anything. I'm bringing a crowbar to defend myself, got it?"

"Oh, we got it," Jack said. He nodded at his friends. A key scraped in the lock. The bolt opened. Kenny stepped into the cell.

"Now!" the three boys cried together. Then they leapt on Kenny. His crowbar wasn't enough to defend himself against the three boys. Soon he was pinned on his stomach, with Nelson and Zeek on his back.

"Let me up!" Kenny shouted.

"So you can turn your monster on us?" Zeek said. "Let me think about it. Um, no."

Nelson and Jack laughed. "I'll go through his pockets," Jack said, "to find a key to free Paul."

Kenny's keychain was easy to find, and soon the boys were free. They held Kenny down while they got ready to go.

"Is everyone ready to run?" Jack asked. He stood in the open doorway. His friends nodded.

"Let me grab that gas can," Paul said. "I filled it before they grabbed me."

The boys headed outside and found Paul's gas. Then they ran off down the road.

- Chapter 9: Running in the Rain -

It was still pouring, harder now. The boys were soaked to the skin in moments. The road was slippery, so they couldn't run as fast as they wanted to.

When Jack tried to really sprint, he slipped and fell into the guardrail. "Ow," he said, struggling to get up.

"We have to keep moving," Paul said nervously. He took his brother by the arm to help him up.

Zeek, clutching his belly, jogged past them. "What's the big hurry?" he said. "Luna and her grandma are out hunting that other werewolf. They won't be looking for us."

A howl filled the night sky.

"But the werewolf might be," Paul said, "if they haven't caught him yet."

Nelson nodded. "Good point," he said. "Let's get moving."

The boys ran on until they came to the overpass where they'd first met Caleb.

"I have to rest a minute," Zeek said. He dropped to the sidewalk, holding his stomach.

"Let me see that," Paul said. "It looks like the bleeding has started again."

"We can't stop now," Jack said as a howl screamed across the sky. "The car isn't much farther. Maybe a hundred yards. We're almost to safety!"

Zeek looked up at him and nodded. "Okay," he said. "I'll try to keep going."

The other boys helped him to his feet, then turned to keep moving. They stopped dead in their tracks.

The young werewolf stood blocking the other side of the overpass. He crouched there, eyeing them, ready to pounce.

"Run!" Jack shouted. The four boys turned back the way they came.

"But the car," Zeek said, gasping for breath. "It's the other way."

"We can't fight that monster," Paul said. "Keep running."

As they came out from the overpass, though, a voice called out from above: "Here he comes."

The boys looked up just as the werewolf leapt at them. From above, a big net fell, catching the werewolf and sending him tumbling to the pavement.

"It's Luna!" Jack said. "She caught Caleb!"

The other boys looked up as Luna stepped to the edge and realized she'd saved her own victims. "It's them!" she said. Her grandma came up beside her.

"Well, don't let them get away," Grandma snapped. She didn't look so kind anymore.

"To the car," Jack said. "We can make it if we run."

The boys ran past the netted werewolf and into the rain. Soon they reached the car.

"Hurry!" Jack said as his brother fumbled with the keys.

The doors opened and the boys climbed in.

"We made it!" Nelson said. The others cheered and laughed.

"I can't believe we're okay," Zeek said. "I can't believe we made it out of Ravens Pass alive."

Paul, smiling, slid his key into the ignition and turned it. Nothing happened. Then he realized the gas can was inside the car — with them, and still full of gas.

Jack laughed. "It's okay," he said. "Go fill the tank. Hurry."

Zeek shook his head as he looked out the rear window. "No way," he said. "Too late."

Jack turned around. Behind the car, smiling at the boys, were Luna and Grandma . . . and a young werewolf on a leash.

Chapter 10: Fever

"We're trapped," Zeek said. "That's it."

"Come out of there and give yourselves up," Luna shouted.

"No way," Jack said, shaking his head. "If we stay in here till the sun comes up, he'll turn back into a normal human, right?"

"That's not for hours," Paul said.

"Then we'll wait for hours," Jack said. "The doors are locked, right?"

They were, but the windows were made of glass.

Luna walked off into the weeds and came back carrying a softball-sized rock. "If you don't come out," she said, "I'll smash the window and let the werewolf boy climb in to get you. Understand?"

"She's serious," Nelson said. "What are we going to do?"

Jack put his hands up. "Wait, Luna," he said. "We'll come out. Just keep the werewolf back, okay?"

"Of course," she said. She nodded at Grandma. The old lady backed away from the car and pulled Caleb with her.

"Okay, I'm unlocking the door," Jack said. He flicked the lock. "Luna, you come open it and we'll climb out."

Luna went to the door and lifted the handle. The moment the door was open, Jack reached out and grabbed her necklace.

"Hey!" Luna snapped, trying to grab it back. She wasn't quick enough.

Jack took the necklace and ran over to Caleb and Grandma. He held the necklace out, toward the werewolf. The monster recoiled and snarled.

"I knew it," Jack said. He spun to his friends. "The charm on this necklace keeps Luna and Grandma safe from the monsters. Grandma has the same thing in her pocket."

Paul jumped out of the car and filled up the tank. Jack stayed at his side, holding out the necklace.

When the tank was full, the boys got back into the car. It started on the first try.

"Let's get out of here," Zeek said.

Jack nodded. He opened his window and held the necklace out to Luna. "Here," he said. "You can have this back." She grabbed the necklace and the car sped away.

"Release Caleb!" Luna shouted. But it was too late. The car was zooming down the highway as fast as Paul could drive.

The drive back home was a long one. Soon Nelson was asleep in the back seat.

"I don't feel so good," Zeek said quietly.

"We're going to get you to a hospital," Paul said. "You'll be okay."

"No," Zeek said. "It's not my stomach. The bleeding stopped."

"Then what's wrong?" Jack said. He turned in his seat. In the dark, he could barely see his friend's face.

"I'm not sure," Zeek said. "I feel feverish. Maybe I'm coming down with something."

"Well, the doctors at the hospital will take care of you," Jack said. "Try not to worry."

Zeek nodded. "Hey, can I use your headphones?" Zeek said. "Nelson's snoring is bugging me."

"Sure," Jack said. He took his mp3 player from the bag at his feet, then held it back toward Zeek.

Zeek leaned forward, and his face caught the light from the dashboard.

Jack dropped the mp3 player and stared at his friend. Then he screamed.

Zeek's nose had grown longer and turned black. His eyes were yellow and fierce. And his face was covered in thick, brown hair.

Case number: 484546588

Date reported: August 29

Crime scene: Gary's Gas, Ravens Pass

Local police: None.

Civilian witnesses: Impossible to say—most of
Ravens Pass. This weekend's witnesses were Zeek
Harbage, age 14; Nelson Robs, age 13; Jack
Kipping, age 14; and Paul Kipping, age 17.
Harbage is now at large.

Disturbance: Established group of werewolves.
This is part of a longterm investigation into the
werewolves of Ravens Pass.

Suspect information: The core group consists of
Edna Canis, age 73; Gary Canis, age 45; Kenny
Henderson, age 19; Caleb Canis, age 16; Luna
Canis, age 14; possible others.

THE FORGOTTEN KID CASE

CASE NOTES:

THIS WAS ONE OF THE MOST FRIGHTENING CASES IN MY CAREER. WEREWOLVES ON THE LOOSE, A TOWN THAT NEEDED TO BE PROTECTED — AND I COULDN'T TELL THE LOCAL POLICE BECAUSE THEY WERE IN ON IT, AT THE TIME.

I KNEW ABOUT THE PROBLEM LONG BEFORE THESE BOYS FROM OUT OF TOWN WERE LURED IN BY THE YOUNGEST WOLF, BUT THIS WAS WHAT I WAS WAITING FOR. OUT-OF-TOWNERS HAVE BEEN DISAPPEARING IN RAVENS PASS FOR YEARS. THIS WAS THE FIRST TIME A NEW ONE WAS BITTEN.

SOMEHOW THESE BOYS MANAGED TO FIGHT OFF THE WEREWOLF THAT THEIR FRIEND TURNED INTO. THEY PUSHED HIM OUT OF THE CAR. THEN THEY DROVE INTO TOWN AND WENT TO THE POLICE. THE POLICE KNEW ABOUT IT, BUT I'M A GOOD LISTENER — I PICKED UP ON TOWN GOSSIP, GOT IN TOUCH WITH THE BOYS, AND THROUGH THEIR STORIES, WAS ABLE TO SMOKE OUT THE WHOLE DEN OF WOLVES.

THE REST IS HISTORY. EXCEPT THAT ONE MISSING KID.

DEAR READER,

THEY ASKED ME TO WRITE ABOUT MYSELF. THE FIRST
THING YOU NEED TO KNOW IS THAT JASON STRANGE IS
NOT MY REAL NAME. IT'S A NAME I'VE TAKEN TO HIDE MY
TRUE IDENTITY AND PROTECT THE PEOPLE I CARE ABOUT.

YOU WOULDN'T BELIEVE THE THINGS I'VE SEEN, WHAT I'VE
WITNESSED. IF PEOPLE KNEW I WAS TELLING THESE STORIES,
SHARING THEM WITH THE WORLD, THEY'D TRY TO GET ME TO
STOP. BUT THESE STORIES NEED TO BE TOLD, AND I'M THE
ONLY ONE WHO CAN TELL THEM.

I CAN'T TELL YOU MANY DETAILS ABOUT MY LIFE. I CAN TELL
YOU I WAS BORN IN A SMALL TOWN AND LIVE IN ONE STILL. I
CAN TELL YOU I WAS A POLICE DETECTIVE HERE FOR TWENTY-
FIVE YEARS BEFORE I RETIRED. I CAN TELL YOU I'M STILL
OUT THERE EVERY DAY AND THAT CRAZY THINGS ARE STILL
HAPPENING.

I'LL LEAVE YOU WITH ONE QUESTION—IS ANY OF THIS TRUE?

JASON STRANGE
RAVENS PASS

Glossary

charm (CHARM)—a small ornament worn on a necklace or bracelet

exhausted (eg-ZAWST-id)—very tired

exposed (ek-SPOHZD)—revealed the truth

fidgeted (FIJ-it-id)—made small quick movements

figure (FIG-yur)—a shape or an outline

guardrail (GARD-rayl)—a rail that prevents people from falling off or being hit by something

ignition (ig-NISH-uhn)—the electrical system of a vehicle that uses power from the battery to start the engine

overpass (OH-vur-pass)—a road or bridge that crosses over another road or a railroad

superstitious (soo-pur-STI-shuhss)—having beliefs about good and bad luck affecting yourself

suspects (suh-SPEKTS)—guesses or supposes

terrorize (TER-uh-rize)—frighten

torrent (TOR-ruhnt)—a violent, fast stream of water

werewolf (WAIR-wulf)—a mythical human who turns into a wolf during the full moon

DISCUSSION QUESTIONS

1. Do you believe in werewolves? Why or why not?

2. If you found out your best friend was a werewolf, what would you do?

3. What was the creepiest part of this book? Explain your answer.

1. Reread the last page of this story. Then write a chapter that continues the story. What happens next?

2. This is a horror story. Write your own horror story.

3. The boys in this book have been on vacation. Write about a trip you'd like to take with your friends. Where would you go? What would you do?